For Matty

A silly story and pictures just for
you

Ruth Finnegan
x x
x

June 2019

The Fantastical Children of Pond Kingdom

A Story retold by Ruth Finnegan

Pictures by Liz Amini-Holmes

Once upon a time in the long long ago there were two children.

One was poor. One was rich. One was very good at sums. The other one was not. But they liked each other a lot. And all the time they were playing together.

Now in this land everyone loved frogs. It was a far away land but there were lots and lots and lots of frogs. There were little green frogs, all hopping around on the grass.

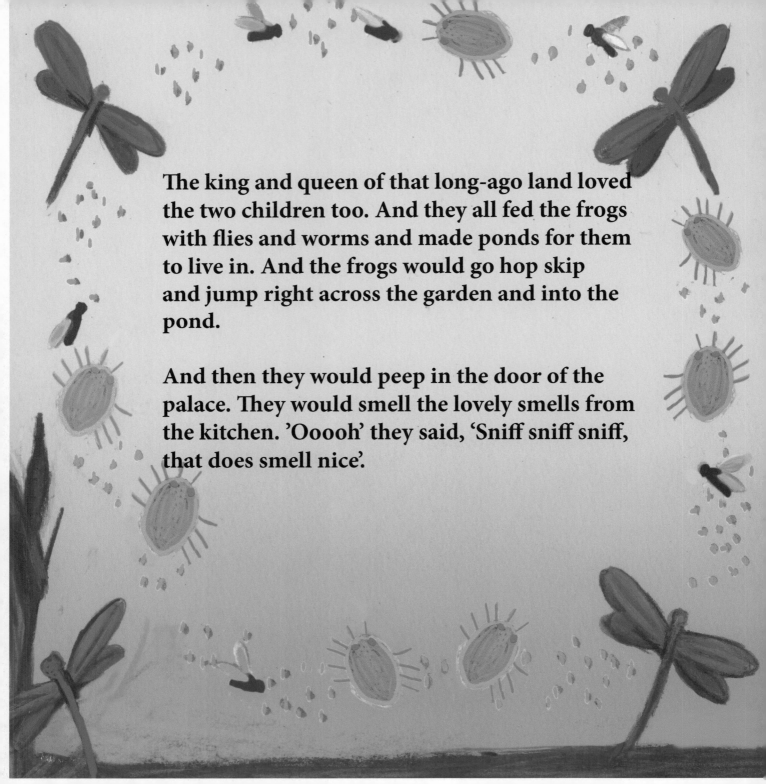

The king and queen of that long-ago land loved the two children too. And they all fed the frogs with flies and worms and made ponds for them to live in. And the frogs would go hop skip and jump right across the garden and into the pond.

And then they would peep in the door of the palace. They would smell the lovely smells from the kitchen. 'Ooooh' they said, 'Sniff sniff sniff, that does smell nice'.

(Did you know that frogs could sniff? No I didn't know that either).

The queen would always say 'Come in little frogs!' Do you think they did No, they DIDN'T.

The little boy frogs said 'I'm too brave to go in there.' (What do you think they meant by that?).

The little girl frogs said 'Our clothes are not pretty enough for a palace, so we won't go in either.' (Weren't they silly!)

But oh oh! What do I see? ONE little frog is peeping round the door.

I don't think the queen can see him, do you? (Yes, it's a little boy frog isn't it? I wonder what he is called).

Look at him!

Well anyway, most of the frogs nev-
er went into the palace.

So that was how it was for a long
long time.

It was like that until the boy and the girl grew up. And the king and queen were very very proud of them, just as if they were their own children, like a real prince and princess (do you know anyone else who is proud of their children even if they are not frogs? Or a prince or princess? Or won't go into the palace?).

Well anyway one day the king said 'All right. You're grown up now. You must go off and do the job of being a king and a queen over a land far away'.
And the queen said the same.

'Will it have frogs in it?' they asked.

The king and the queen looked at each other. 'Yes, perhaps' they said. 'And you must be very very kind to them or you will not be a proper king or queen'.

'Can we go together? The two of us together?' they asked.

'No' said the king, 'you must be very brave and go all on your own or you will not be a real king and queen. Kings and queens have to be very very brave even if they are alone. And then you can join up. After you have been brave'.

'YES ' said the queen. 'But queens and kings need someone to help them. And love them. And make them a good kind king and queen, very kind. That is the rule. So you can each take ONE little frog with you'.

'And our cuddlies?' they asked.

The queen shook her head. The king shook his head too. 'Kings and queens don't have cuddlies,' they said. 'A little frog would be MUCH better'.

So then all the little green frogs jumped up and down and up and down. (Can you do that?) 'Me, me, me, ME, ME', they all shouted. Then they shouted again in case the queen was not able to hear them (can you? Yes, like that, just like that!).

Then they shouted again, specially to the queen. They liked her a lot. And oh yes, they liked the king too.

So the queen shut her eyes and said 'All right, the first one I touch.' Guess what happened. One little frog jumped right onto her lap, yes right up and tickled her under her chin. So the queen laughed and said 'All right little frog, you are the one.'

But the king said 'Hey hey hey all of you, what about the other child then? He must have a little frog too'.

So he shut his eyes. And guess what happened! Yes, just the same thing.

Only this time the king laughed and laughed so much that he fell off. His chair. And the little frog fell off too, RIGHT onto the ground.

And you know what happens when frogs fall onto the ground, they just go hop and skip and a jump. So J-U-M-P! UP it went onto the king's chin and then, JUMP, onto his head!

So that little frog was allowed to go too.

So the boy and girl went off. They missed the king. And they missed the queen too. But they had their special little frogs to look after. And to look after them.

And guess what? They found lots and lots and lots of little frogs in their kingdoms. And those little frogs were green too and hopped and skipped and jumped right up to the palace door. But - sssh – sometimes they came in.

And one day the boy and girl met each other by the pond. Wow!

'Hullo you!' said one.

And one day the boy and girl met each other by the pond.
Wow!

'Hullo you!' said one.

So do you know what they did?

Yes, you've guessed right. They said they would to join their two kingdoms together so they could play with each other again.

So now they were the new king and queen and they were
very kind to all the frogs just like they had been told to do.
(Do you? Yes, don't all shout at once!)

After a long time they had their own children.

'But what will we call them?' they asked.

The new queen said, 'I would like a frog name'.

The new king thought and thought. Then he thought again. 'I don't know' he said.

He asked his friends and they thought and thought too. 'We don't know', they said (perhaps you know? But don't tell them yet. Sssssh, it's a secret. Sssssh).

KISS

ME!

Balestier Press
71-75 Shelton Street, London WC2H 9JQ
www.balestier.com

The Fantastical Children of Pond Kingdom

First published in English by Balestier Press in 2019

ISBN 978 1 911221 23 4

Lightning Source UK Ltd.
Milton Keynes UK
UKHW052251290519
343547UK00002BA/2/P

* 9 7 8 1 9 1 1 2 2 1 1 0 4 *